VISITOR

THE COLOR FACTORY

NAME

_____

AGE

_____

OCCUPATION

_____

For the most colorful people I know, my nieces
and nephews: Marly, Derek, Brooke, Henry, and Oliver
—ET

To Julen
—DF

little bee books

An imprint of Bonnier Publishing USA
251 Park Avenue South, New York, NY 10010
Text copyright © 2018 by Eric Telchin
Illustrations copyright © 2018 by Diego Funck
All rights reserved, including the right of reproduction
in whole or in part in any form. Little Bee Books is a
trademark of Bonnier Publishing USA, and associated colophon
is a trademark of Bonnier Publishing USA.
Manufactured in China   LEO 0318
First Edition   10 9 8 7 6 5 4 3 2 1
Library of Congress Cataloging-in-Publication Data
Names: Telchin, Eric, author. | Funck, Diego, illustrator.
Title: The Color Factory / by Eric Telchin; illustrated by Diego Funck.
Description: First edition. | New York, NY: Little Bee Books, [2018]
Summary: Panda, Penguin, and Zebra lead a tour of the Color Factory,
where only twelve perfect colors are approved, but things go wrong and the
reader must help set them right. | Identifiers: LCCN 2017023553
Subjects: | CYAC: Color—Fiction. | Factories—Fiction. | Animals—Fiction.
Classification: LCC PZ7.T2355 Col 2018 | DDC [E]—dc23
LC record available at https://lccn.loc.gov/2017023553
ISBN 978-1-4998-0556-7

littlebeebooks.com
bonnierpublishingusa.com

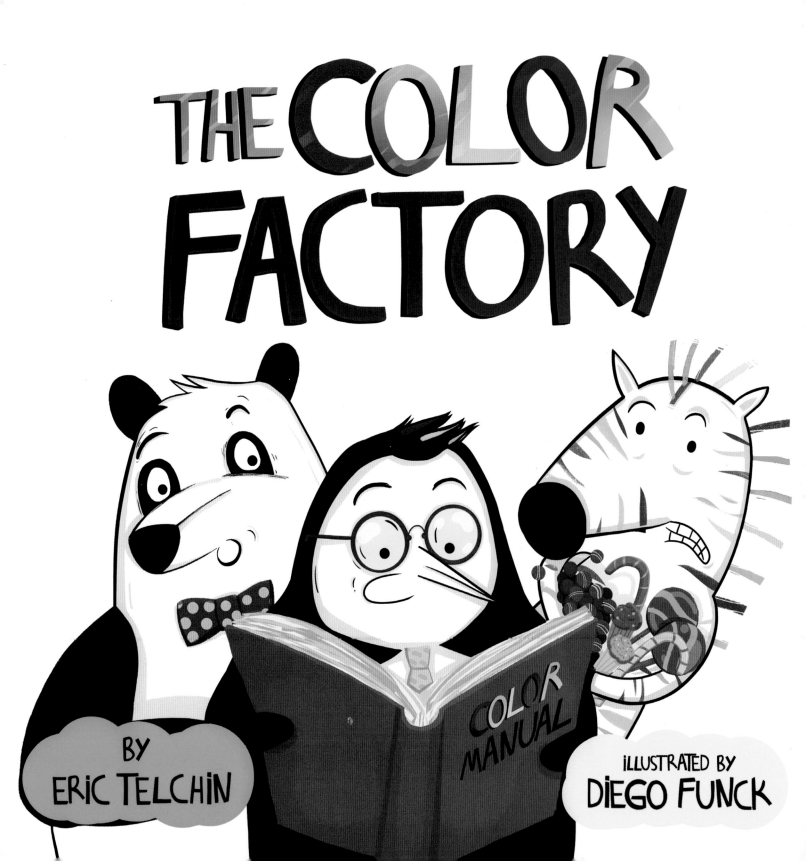

THE COLOR FACTORY

BY
ERIC TELCHIN

ILLUSTRATED BY
DIEGO FUNCK

COLOR MANUAL

We create colors here. We use very strict formulas so we can make these colors *perfect*. Once the colors are approved, we apply them to all sorts of things!
We also make books! In fact, the book you're reading *right now* is filled with factory-approved colors. Simply turn the page and we'll start the tour!
FAST-GROWING ROSE SEEDS
Factory-Approved Rose
18 COLORS
Factory-Approved Canary Yellow

And remember those fast-growing rose seeds? Well, they certainly did grow fast. We're copying their color to make Factory-Approved Rose.
Next, we're going to create Factory-Approved Orange. You can probably guess how we're going to do that!

That's right! Factory-Approved Orange is made from Fire Engine Red and Canary Yellow.
Now that the Perfect Color Replicator has matched these two colors, we just need to mix them together. Can you help us?

Perfect! Great job! We approve! The formula for Factory-Approved Orange works every time.
That's because our formulas are perfect!
Because our colors are perfect! Now let's move on to the Creature Colorization Room.

This egg needs to be colored with Factory-Approved Robin's Egg Blue.
But first we need to mix that color. Simply follow the formula from the *Color Manual*: three taps of Factory-Approved Sky Blue, a quick rub of Factory-Approved Grass Green, and a squiggle of Factory-Approved Cloud White.
PRESS HERE
Use your finger to tap, rub, and squiggle. Then press this button.
PERFEC
ICATO

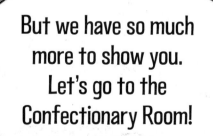

The Confectionary Room is the most colorful, most delicious, most *perfect* room in the whole Color Factory.
But we have treats that still need to be colored.
Could you help us?
3-D ICE-CREAM PRINTER

Since you're doing such a perfect job, we'd like you to color this lollipop.

Use your finger to pull Factory-Approved Robin's Egg Blue onto it. And drag some Factory-Approved Cotton Candy Pink, too.
Be careful not to mix the colors as you apply them to the lollipop! This is very important!

NOT FACTORY APPROVED
This color is not in the *Color Manual*! It's not a factory-approved color!
WHE
EEEEE
COLOR MANUAL

We do not approve!
WHEEEEEE
You have to help us remove this color from the factory! Please rub the color off the page!

Uh-oh . . .
PERFECT COLOR
Now it's worse! This non-factory-approved color is changing everything!
COLOR MANUAL
Don't worry. The *Color Manual* will tell us what to do.

COLOR MANUAL

INDEX

PUSH HERE FOR INSTRUCTIONS

Quick! Push the button!

ADDING COLOR
TO THE COLOR FACTORY:

If you removed
factory-approved colors
from the Color Factory,
you're in big, **BIG** trouble.
You better ask someone for help!

Uh-oh . . .
Now there are even *more* non-factory-approved colors!
NOT FACTORY APPROVED
We'll have to check the *Color Manual* again to find a solution.

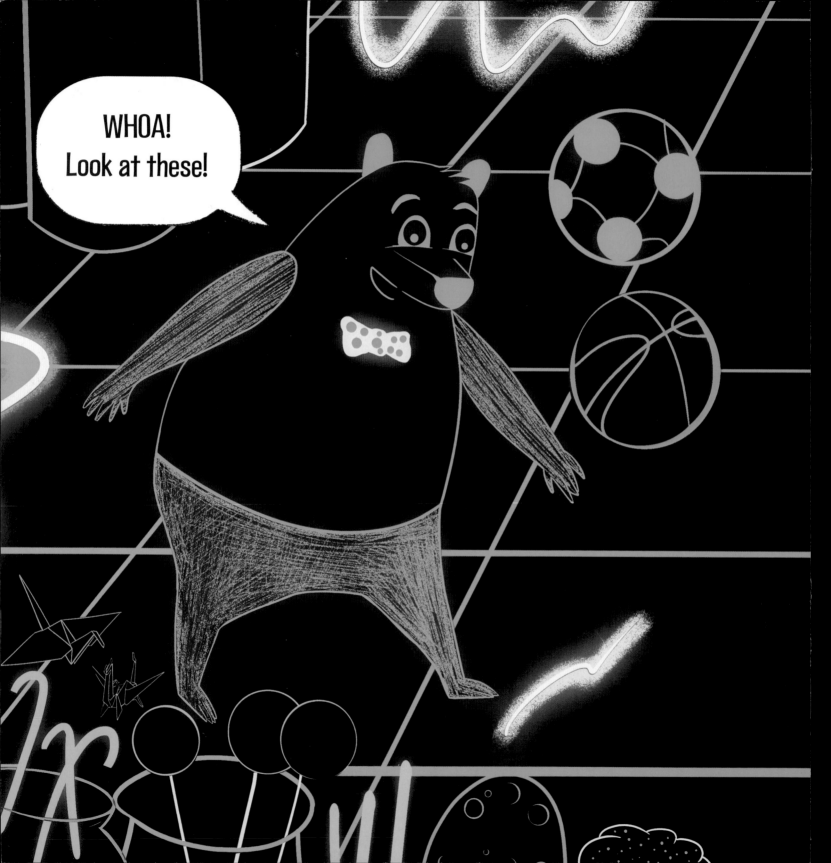

ON
Reader! Turn the power back on! Now we don't need to close the Color Factory!
These colors are factory approved!